BALTIMORE, June 25.

Yesterday the ingenious PETER CARNES, Esq; made his curious ÆROSTATIC EXPERIMENTS, within the Limits of this Town, in the Presence of a numerous and respectable Congress of People, whom the Fame of his superb BALLOON had drawn together from the East, West, North and South, who, generally, appeared highly delighted with the awful Grandeur of so novel a Scene, as a large Globe making repeated *Voyages* into the airy Regions, which Mr. CARNES's Machine actually performed, in a Manner that reflected Honour on his Character as a Man of Genius, and could not fail to inspire solemn and exalted Ideas in every reflecting Mind.——Ambition, on this Occasion, so fired the youthful Heart of a Lad (only 13 Years old!) of the Name of *Edward Warren*) that he bravely embarked as a Volunteer on the last *Trip* into the Air, and behaved with the steady Fortitude of an *old Voyager.*—The " gazing Multitude below" wafted to him their loud Applause, the Receipt of which, as he was " soaring aloof," he politely acknowledged by a significant Wave of his Hat.—When he returned to our terrene Element, he met with a Reward, from some of the Spectators, which had a *solid*, instead of an *airy*, Foundation, and of a *Species* which is ever acceptable to the Residents of this *lower World.*

NAVAL-OFFICE, BALTIMORE.

Inward Entries. Sloop William, E. Dillingham, from North-Carolina ; Ship Juffraw Jacoba Maria Lucia Theresia, J. Albert, Barcelona ; Ship Patience, D. Campbell, St. Martin's.

Cleared Outwards. Schooner Sally, D. Jones, for Newbern ; Ship Swift, T. Pamp, London ; Sloop St. John, E. Peters, Curacoa.

The Amazing Air Balloon

Jean Van Leeuwen / Pictures by *Marco Ventura*

Phyllis Fogelman Books New York

For Bruce—J.V.L.
In memory of my grandmother Giulia Sommacal—M.V.

Published by Phyllis Fogelman Books
An imprint of Penguin Putnam Books for Young Readers
345 Hudson Street
New York, New York 10014

Text copyright © 2003 by Jean Van Leeuwen
Pictures copyright © 2003 by Marco Ventura
All rights reserved
Designed by Nancy R. Leo-Kelly
Text set in Caslon 540
Manufactured in China on acid-free paper
1 3 5 7 9 10 8 6 4 2

Library of Congress Cataloging-in-Publication Data
Van Leeuwen, Jean.
The amazing air balloon / Jean Van Leeuwen ; pictures by Marco Ventura.
p. cm.
Edward Warren was the first person to go up in a balloon in America on June 24, 1784.
Summary: In this story based on true events,
a thirteen-year-old apprentice takes the first manned hot-air balloon flight in
America and gains new insight into life's possibilities.
ISBN 0-8037-2258-3
[1. Hot air balloons—Fiction. 2. Balloon ascensions—Fiction.] I. Ventura, Marco, ill. II. Title.
PZ7.V275 Ap 2003 [Fic]—dc21 2001050154

The art for this book was prepared using oil paint on gessoed Fabriano paper.

"Some suppose flying to be now invented; since men may be supported in the air, nothing is wanted but some light, handy instruments to give and direct motion."
                                                                            —*Benjamin Franklin*

"All the people are running after air globes . . . The invention of them may have many consequences, and who knows but travelers may hereafter literally pass from country to country on the wings of the wind."
                                                  —*John Jay, First Chief Justice of the U.S. Supreme Court*

*N*ever will I forget that April day.

My master, Mr. Sloane, was busy shoeing an ox when we heard shouting. I looked out and beheld a great wonder.

It was a paper globe as tall as a man. Attached beneath was a fire-burning device. Mr. Carnes, the proprietor of the Indian Queen Tavern, was feeding straw into the fire. The globe puffed out like a sail in a fresh wind.

"An air balloon!" I exclaimed.

Could it really be? We had heard talk of these marvels lately being launched, but that was across the sea in Paris, France.

"Look," said Mr. Sloane. "It is rising!" Now the balloon was higher than Mr. Carnes's head. Now higher than the tavern roof. Higher than the trees.

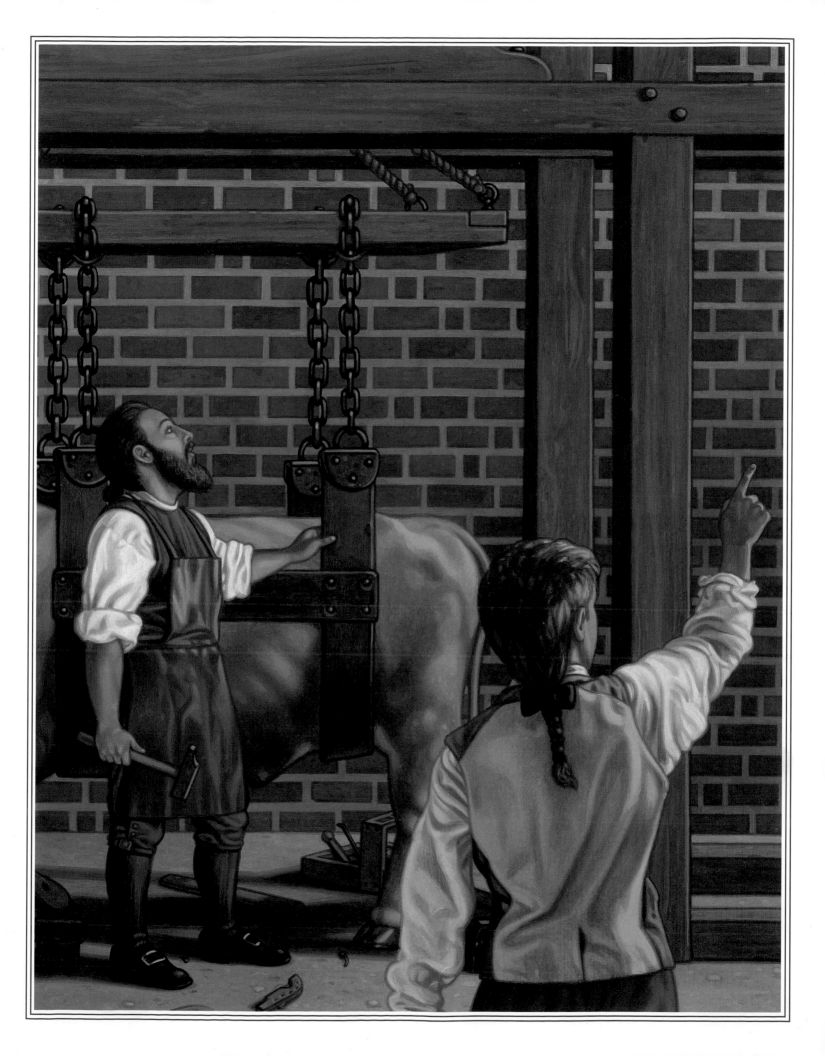

"Hurrah!" cheered men from the docks along the river.

Then, very gently, the balloon began to descend.

Oh, what a wondrous thing it must be, I thought, to fly through the air.

From that day on, I thought of little but air balloons. What made them rise? I wondered. How high could they fly? Might it be possible to steer one like a ship? And could a man ascend and come safely down?

Mr. Sloane just shook his head when I asked him. "If we were meant to fly," he said, "we would have been given wings by our Creator."

But Mr. Carnes meant to fly someday. My friend Robert, the stable boy at the Indian Queen Tavern, told me so. All that spring Mr. Carnes kept testing balloons.

One rose as high as the church, then settled on top of a house and rolled off to the ground.

One became entangled in the branches of an oak tree.

One caught fire and made a spectacular blaze in midair.

After that, some in our small village of Bladensburg called Peter Carnes a fool. But he just laughed good-naturedly.

"We will see, gentlemen," he said. And he built another balloon.

This one was his largest yet. It was thirty-five feet around and made of many-colored silk, with ropes to tether it to earth. A round stove provided the fire, and a basket large enough for two passengers hung beneath.

When I saw it, I knew he intended to fly.

A great longing came over me then. If only it could be me who soared up into the sky, free as a bird to ride wherever the wind took me.

But that could not be. I was bound to earth. Bound to the hard labor of a blacksmith's apprentice until I was twenty-one. I had not chosen this life. It was because I was an orphan. Still, I could not escape.

Then, in June, came amazing news.

"Mr. Carnes is to exhibit his balloon in Baltimore," Robert told me. "On June twenty-fourth. See, Edward, it is all here in this newspaper."

I had not had much schooling since my father died fighting for liberty with General Washington, and my mother of a fever soon after. But lying in my loft bed that night, I puzzled out the words. Yes, it was really true.

In the shops, along the docks, everyone was talking of it. Large crowds gathered to watch each time Mr. Carnes tried out his new air balloon.

On June 9, Thomas Rogers, the miller, came bursting into the shop. "The balloon has escaped!" he cried.

Outside, people were running and horses galloping. I looked at Mr. Sloane. He nodded. "Go ahead, boy," he said.

I followed the crowd, past the countinghouse, the schoolhouse, out beyond town. There was Mr. Carnes, red-faced and shouting, on his big gray horse. But where was the balloon?

Then someone pointed. It was just rising above a ridge, so high and far away, it looked like a dot in the sky.

"It will come down," cried Mr. Carnes, "when the fire dies out."

We chased that balloon over hills and streams and farmers' fields until at last it began to descend. It landed, barely missing a barn, in the middle of a tobacco field. Amazingly, it was only a little damaged.

"I will fly it again tomorrow," Mr. Carnes proclaimed.

Only a few days remained before the exhibition. Mr. Carnes planned one last test flight. And this time, everyone said, he would go up with it.

Never before had a man flown in a balloon. Not here in America, though it had been done in France. Benjamin Franklin himself had seen it. First a duck, sheep, and rooster had been sent up, and later two men. I had read about it in the old newspapers Robert brought me.

The largest crowd yet gathered at the edge of town.

"Will he really go up?" everyone was asking. Mr. Carnes was such a big man. Could his balloon lift all that weight?

The balloon had been filled in a wooded area. Now it had to be moved to a field. Six men held its tethers. Robert and I ran after them, hoping to help.

"Hold it fast," Mr. Carnes cautioned as they crossed a road.

Just as he spoke, a gust of wind caught the balloon. It brushed against a fence. One man fell, losing hold of his rope.

"Catch it!"

Robert leaped and seized the rope. I caught the end, holding it tight.

"Good work, boys!" Mr. Carnes clapped Robert on the back.

But the hoop that surrounded the balloon was broken. Though he could still send it up, Mr. Carnes dared not go with it.

As it rose above the trees, the crowd buzzed with disappointment.

"Bring it down and I will go up!" one man shouted.

Mr. Carnes waved for quiet. "The balloon is so damaged that it could catch fire," he said. "I cannot risk it. But come to Baltimore in five days' time."

More than anything, I longed to be in Baltimore for his exhibition. But that was thirty miles away. And I was not free to go. My life was the smoky fire, the smell of hot iron, the ring of hammer on anvil.

The next day Robert came to the shop. "I am to go to Baltimore," he told me happily. "To take care of the horses. Mr. Carnes himself has asked me."

Robert was my good friend. But, oh, how I envied him at that moment.

At last it was the day before the exhibition. Outside the Indian Queen Tavern, wagons were being loaded. I watched as men lifted the huge bundle of silk into one wagon, the heavy stove into another.

A sharp ache ran through me, and I turned away.

Minutes later I heard a horse whinny, a rumble of voices. Then Robert was standing in the doorway, breathless.

"A man has been hurt in the loading. His leg looks to be broken. Mr. Carnes asks if Edward can take his place."

I hardly dared breathe as Mr. Sloane put down his hammer.

"I believe I can spare you," he said with a smile.

"Oh, thank you, sir!"

The moment Robert and I were outside, we let out such whoops of excitement, the horses nearly bolted. I was going to Baltimore!

Never had I seen so many houses, all built around a bay. And paved streets. And fine, bustling shops. And everywhere the talk was of Peter Carnes and his amazing air balloon.

The launch was to take place in a wooded park north of town. Here a tall fence had been built, with guards placed all around it. Only those who bought tickets were allowed inside.

Early in the morning a crowd began to gather. It grew and grew. Soon the fenced area was full. Yet still more kept arriving.

"Baltimore has gone balloon mad!" I heard one gentleman tell his lady.

At last Mr. Carnes rose to address the crowd. "Some may wonder," he said, "of what use is an air balloon. Is it merely a toy for public amusement? My reply, like that of Benjamin Franklin, is 'What is the use of a newborn babe?' I predict that many uses will be found. A balloon can teach us about the upper reaches of the atmosphere. It might be used as a signal, or to lift heavy weights over mountains, or to cross deserts. It may even convince men of the folly of war. For who can defend against a balloon-borne invasion force that might land anywhere?"

Then he gave the signal for the balloon to ascend.

"Ahhhh!" sighed the crowd as it began to rise.

Like a live creature, the balloon tugged to pull free of earth. Then it soared into a bright blue sky—a hundred feet, two hundred. If it hadn't been tethered, I thought, it might have risen above the clouds.

Four more times that day the balloon went up and was brought down. Now came the last ascent. Would Mr. Carnes go with it this time?

The question traveled through the crowd in whispers and murmurs.

"I don't think he dares," Robert whispered to me. "I heard one of his men say he has tried, but the balloon would not lift his weight."

Finally a man shouted out, "Will you go aloft, sir?"

Mr. Carnes hesitated. Robert must be right, I thought.

Then I found myself moving through the crowd. I stepped up next to Mr. Carnes. My heart hammering so I could hardly speak, I said, "I will go."

"Are you sure?" he asked. I nodded, and everyone burst into cheers.

As if in a dream, I stepped into the basket. The ropes were let out, and I felt myself rising. Or was it the earth that was falling? Looking down, I saw a circle of smiling, uplifted faces. Mr. Carnes was dancing about like a great grinning bear. Robert was waving. I took off my hat and waved back.

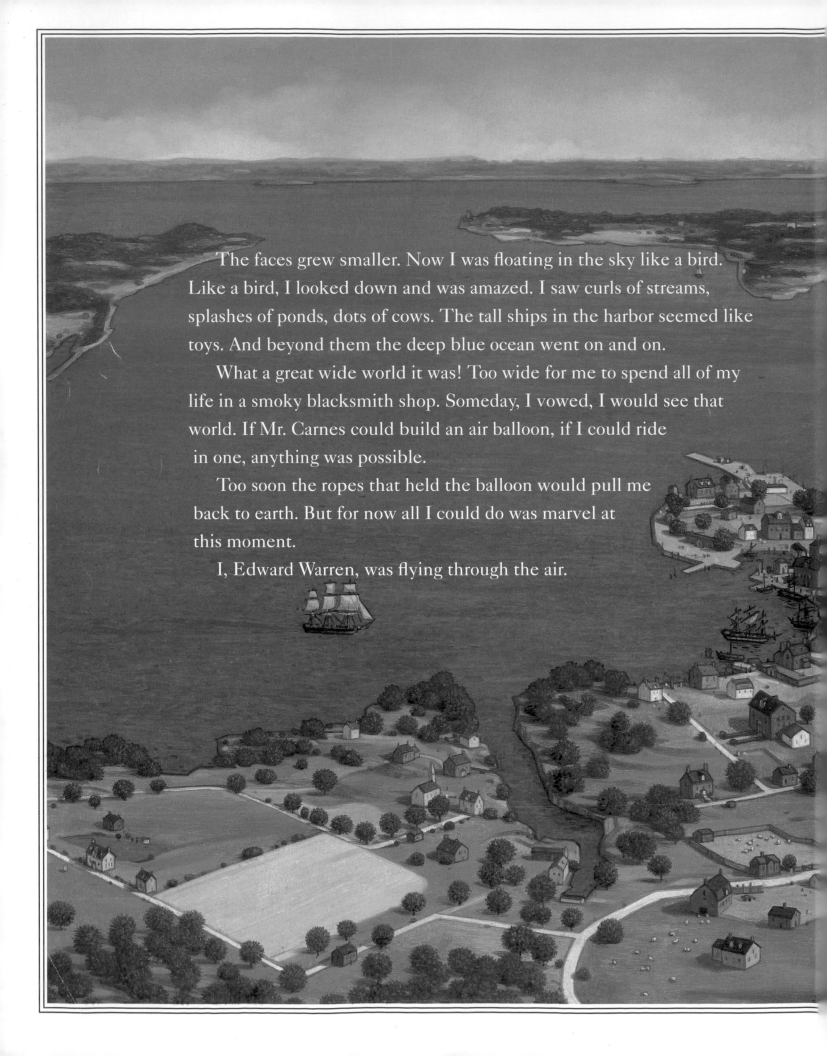

The faces grew smaller. Now I was floating in the sky like a bird. Like a bird, I looked down and was amazed. I saw curls of streams, splashes of ponds, dots of cows. The tall ships in the harbor seemed like toys. And beyond them the deep blue ocean went on and on.

What a great wide world it was! Too wide for me to spend all of my life in a smoky blacksmith shop. Someday, I vowed, I would see that world. If Mr. Carnes could build an air balloon, if I could ride in one, anything was possible.

Too soon the ropes that held the balloon would pull me back to earth. But for now all I could do was marvel at this moment.

I, Edward Warren, was flying through the air.

Author's Note

*I*n the years just following the American Revolution, a surprising craze gripped the people of Europe. It began in France, where in 1783 two brothers, Joseph and Jacques Étienne Montgolfier, built and flew the first hot-air balloon. Soon balloons were being flown everywhere. Scientists and daredevils competed to build the largest one, to fly the farthest, to be the first to carry human passengers.

Benjamin Franklin, in Paris at the time, wrote home enthusiastically about this new device. Experiments with small paper balloons began in Philadelphia. And in the spring of 1784, the leading scientists of the city made plans to build an enormous, elegant balloon capable of carrying a man aloft.

The historic first flight took place on June 24, 1784. But the balloon was not one built by distinguished scientists. It was built by a little-known tavern keeper from a small village outside Baltimore, Peter Carnes. And the first man to go aloft in a balloon in America was not a man at all, but a thirteen-year-old boy named Edward Warren.

Unfortunately, nothing is known about Edward Warren except his name and age. After his brief moment in the historical spotlight, he disappeared from sight. In this story, therefore, I have had to imagine his background and how he happened to be a participant in Peter Carnes's historic flight. All that we actually know comes from a newspaper account of the time: "He bravely embarked as a volunteer on the last trip into the air, and behaved with the steady fortitude of an old voyager. The gazing multitude below wafted to him their loud applause, the receipt of which . . . he politely acknowledged by a significant wave of his hat."

As for Peter Carnes, he attempted one more balloon flight a month later in Philadelphia. This time he did go up himself. However, as his balloon was ascending inside a prison yard, it was blown against a wall. Mr. Carnes was dropped, uninjured, to the ground, while the balloon kept rising until it burst into flames. After this misadventure Peter Carnes gave up ballooning and became a lawyer in South Carolina and Georgia. He died in 1794 at the age of forty-five.

☞ American Æroftatic Balloon.

"*On vent'rous Wing in queft of Praife I go,*
"*And leave the gazing Multitude below.*"

WILL be exhibited, in a field near Baltimore, on Thurf-day, the 24th inftant, if fair, if not, the next fair day, at eight o'clock in the morning, or at five in the evening, and fo on till the exhibition takes place, an

Æroftatic Balloon,

nearly 35 feet diameter, with a fplendid Chariot fufpended at the bottom, fitted for the reception of two perfons, in which the fubfcriber purpofes to afcend above the clouds, after a fhort lecture on the great ufes to which this important difcovery may be applied, for the convenience and delight of human life, and the method of afcertaining the height, velocity and direction of thofe curious ærial Globes, both by fea and land, in the darkeft nights.

A large field, with a high fence, is marked out, and will be guarded on all fides with fire-arms; the centinels being intereft-ed in the exhibition, will be juftifiable in taking the life of any perfon who attempts to force his way into the field, as no per-fon will be admitted but by prefenting a ticket at the gates. Should any perfon, notwithftanding the guards, fteal into the field, a fuit will be commenced inftantly againft him for Ten Pounds.----As the fubfcriber has made his experiments in the prefence of Mr. *Sydebotham*, Mr. *Diggs*, Mr. *Miller*, Mr. *Rofs*, Mr. *Tolforth*, and many other Gentlemen of *Bladenfburg*, who will certify their friends in different parts of the country, no more need be faid refpecting the fuccefs of the exhibition.————
TICKETS may be had of Mr. DANIEL GRANT, at the Fountain-Inn, and at the feveral Coffee-Houfes, in *Baltimore-Town.*

Price of Tickets for the firft place *Two Dollars*, and for the fecond place *Ten Shillings* each. The money that may be re-ceived at the feveral Places laft-mentioned, will be put into the hands of Mr. DANIEL GRANT, which will be returned by him, provided the exhibition does not take place to the en-tire fatisfaction of the fpectators.

PETER CARNES.

Baltimore, June 14. 1784.